Race to the North Pole

Ahoy, mateys!

Set sail for a brand-new adventure with the

PUPPY 🏴‍☠️ PIRATES

Puppy Pirates

Super Special #3

Race to the North Pole

by Erin Soderberg
illustrations by Russ Cox

A STEPPING STONE BOOK™
Random House 🏠 New York

For all the kids who have read and shared
Puppy Pirates with friends and classmates—
this magical adventure is for you!
I hope you have as much fun reading it
as I had writing it. —E.S.

Text copyright © 2018 by Erin Soderberg Downing and Robin Wasserman
Cover art copyright © 2018 by Luz Tapia
Interior illustrations copyright © 2018 by Russ Cox

All rights reserved. Published in the United States by Random House
Children's Books, a division of Penguin Random House LLC, New York.

Random House and the colophon are registered trademarks and A Stepping
Stone Book and the colophon are trademarks of Penguin Random House LLC.

Visit us on the Web!
SteppingStonesBooks.com
rhcbooks.com

Educators and librarians, for a variety of teaching tools, visit us at
RHTeachersLibrarians.com

Library of Congress Cataloging-in-Publication Data
Names: Soderberg, Erin, author. | Cox, Russ, illustrator.
Title: Race to the North Pole / by Erin Soderberg ; illustrated by Russ Cox.
Description: New York : Random House, [2018] | Series: Puppy Pirates.
Super special ; #3 | "A Stepping Stone book." | Summary: "Wally and the
Puppy Pirates compete in a dogsled race at the North Pole" —Provided by
publisher.
Identifiers: LCCN 2017048892 | ISBN 978-0-525-57920-5 (trade) |
ISBN 978-0-525-57922-9 (ebook)
Subjects: | CYAC: Dogs—Fiction. | Pirates—Fiction. | Dogsledding—Fiction. |
Christmas—Fiction. | Adventure and adventurers—Fiction. |
North Pole—Fiction.
Classification: LCC PZ7.S685257 Rac 2018 | DDC [Fic]—dc23

Printed in the United States of America
10 9 8 7 6 5 4 3 2 1
First Edition

This book has been officially leveled by using the F&P Text Level Gradient™
Leveling System.

✕ CONTENTS

North Pole
Adventures Shop

Candy Cane
Forest

Gumdrop
Trail

NORTH POLE

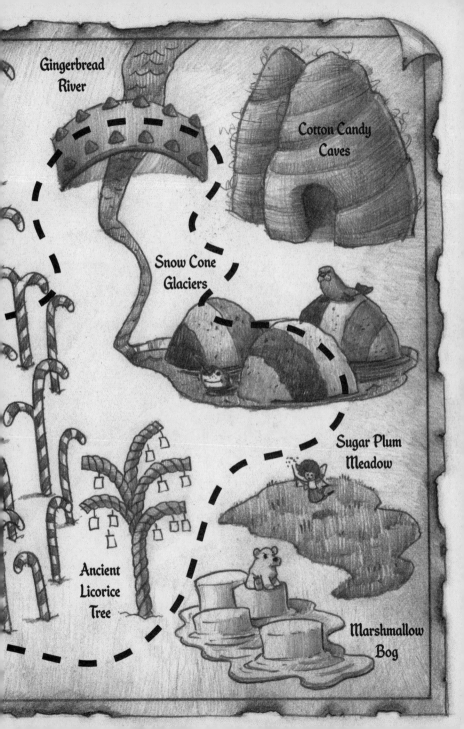

Gingerbread
River

Cotton Candy
Caves

Snow Cone
Glaciers

Sugar Plum
Meadow

Ancient
Licorice
Tree

Marshmallow
Bog

1

Splashing Through the Snow

"Splashing through the snow, off our pirate ship—let's go!" Captain Red Beard sang joyfully as he leaped across the deck of the *Salty Bone*. The gruff puppy pirate captain was in a very good mood. He and his crew had been sailing north for days and days. But they were finally here: the North Pole! It was time for a treasure hunt at the top of the world. Nothing made the captain happier than hunting for treasure.

As a team of pups dropped the anchor,

Captain Red Beard howled out another verse. "We're on an icy quest, for a special treasure—" The shaggy terrier stopped. He scratched one of his reddish ears. "Hmmm," he said. "What rhymes with *quest*?"

A soft golden retriever puppy named Wally barked, "*Chest,* sir? We're on an icy quest, for a special *treasure chest*?"

"*Quest* and *chest* don't rhyme, little Walty!" Captain Red Beard chuckled. "Silly pup."

Wally was pretty sure *chest* and *quest* did rhyme. But he didn't like to argue with Captain Red Beard. On the *Salty Bone,* the captain was always right—even when he wasn't.

The crew lowered the gangplank onto a snowy dock. As soon as it was safe, all the puppy pirates raced ashore. Though life at sea was jolly, it always felt good to leap and bound and run free on land.

Wally's best friend, a human boy called

Henry, scooped up a handful of snow. He packed it into a tight ball. Then he tossed it into the air for Wally to chase after. Soon everyone was playing fetch with the snow! But after a few minutes, the pups slowed down to sniff and snuff. It was exciting to have the chance to explore a strange, new world.

Far off in the distance, Wally could see the edge of a small village. Near the docks there was nothing but snow, snow, and more snow! Usually, the puppy pirates' adventures took them through tropical waters. But this trip was already full of wonderful new sights. They had sailed past icebergs and white-capped mountains. Now soft snowflakes swirled in the air around them. The air was so crisp that every time he took a deep breath, Wally felt like he might sneeze.

"Here, pups!" Red Beard called out. "Gather around." The puppy pirates bounded over to hear what their captain had to say.

As soon as he stopped running, Wally noticed just how chilly it was. Many of his short-haired mates had to huddle together to stay warm. The pug twins squeezed into the warm space under Wayne the Great Dane's belly. Spike the bulldog was busy playing blanket tug-of-war

with his best mate, a tiny Boston terrier named
Humphrey. Einstein, a clumsy wiener dog, was
trying to squirm into a plaid sweater.

Wally lay down in the snow and chewed at his paws. It was fun to bite at the tiny balls of ice stuck between his paw pads. Even though his feet felt a little cold, Wally's body was warm and cozy. At times like this he was glad he had so much warm fur!

"Welcome to the North Pole!" Captain Red Beard barked to his crew. "As you all know, we have sailed through icy waters to run in the Great Ice Race. Teams of pups have come from all over the world to compete, because the winner of the Great Ice Race wins the *greatest treasure of all!*"

"Treasure! Treasure! Treasure!" chanted the puppy pirates.

Curly, the first mate, barked for order. The poufy mini poodle called out, "But there is a catch: the rules say we can only enter one team of six pups in the race."

"What is this hoodly-toodly nonsense? Only *six* pups?" howled the captain. He started to count his crew. "But we have one, two, three, forty-six, nineteen, eleventy . . . fifty-two on our crew! Fifty-two is more than six. That is a problem."

"Every problem has a solution. Right, Captain?" Curly said, nodding. "And *you*, Captain, have come up with the perfect solution. A plan."

"Yes, of course!" Captain Red Beard said uncertainly. "I have a great plan. Remind me, what is my plan again?"

Curly faced the crew and said, "We have decided to hold tryouts to find the fastest runners on our crew. The five quickest pups will get to run with Captain Red Beard in the Great Ice Race."

"Tryouts!" Captain Red Beard said. "Yes, that is exactly what I was thinking. The first five pups to reach the finish line will be on my team. The rest of you will cheer us on."

Wally *loved* to run. He was very fast. He glanced around at his crewmates. There were many speedy and strong pups. Could Wally finish in the top five and earn the chance to run with his captain in the Great Ice Race?

Curly howled, "The starting line is here." Then she lifted a paw and pointed away from the village. Across a huge snowy field, Wally could just barely see a box. "On the other side of this field is a crate filled with steak. The crate marks the finish line. This isn't just a race for a spot on Captain Red Beard's team . . . it's also a race to your dinner! Ready, set—"

"Avast!" Captain Red Beard cried out. "Before you race, I want to remind everyone where we are." The captain spoke very seriously. "This is the home of the Great Ice Race. It's also the

Christmas capital of the world. And Christmas is only days away!"

The pups yipped and woofed. Wally wagged his tail. Christmas was always fun. But Christmas at the North Pole? That might be the most fun of all!

Captain Red Beard said, "At the North Pole, it's very important to do Christmas right. Who knows what that means?"

Many pups started to bark an answer. But the captain barked louder than all of them. "*I* know. Doing Christmas right means *giving* . . . your dear ol' captain the right gifts. This season is all about *me* getting *exactly* what I want. And what I want is to win that shiny, sparkly treasure!" He stomped his paw on the ground. "But also . . ."

The captain pulled out a very long piece of parchment. He cleared his throat and read the list of all the things he wanted for Christmas:

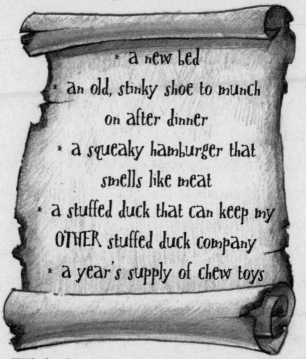

* a new bed
* an old, stinky shoe to munch on after dinner
* a squeaky hamburger that smells like meat
* a stuffed duck that can keep my OTHER stuffed duck company
* a year's supply of chew toys

While the captain rambled on, the rest of the crew chattered about some of the presents *they* wanted. Wally didn't really have anything on his own wish list. He had Henry and his puppy pirate family. He had a home on the *Salty Bone* and a life of adventure on the high seas. What more could a puppy need?

But Wally *did* want to find a great gift for Henry. Henry was the best friend ever, so Wally wanted to get him the best *gift* ever. Something big! Something shiny! Something *perfect*.

He just didn't know what.

As Captain Red Beard flipped over his list to read the other side, Curly stepped forward. She let out one sharp bark to get his attention. When that didn't work, she whispered in his ear. But the captain was so focused on his gift list that he didn't notice her—or the setting sun.

Finally, Curly barked, "Arrrrf! Shiver me timbers, let's get on with the tryouts, Captain. It's getting late."

"What?" Captain Red Beard looked up from his parchment. "Oh, right, the *race!*" He lifted a paw and pointed across the snowy landscape. "Are you ready, puppy pirates? Get set . . . GO!"

Steak Race

Wally and the other puppy pirates barked and yipped as they raced each other across the snowy field. At first, the whole pack stayed close together. But soon the quickest dogs began to pull away from the group.

Wayne galloped through the snow on his long legs. *"Arrrr-oooo!"* The huge Great Dane whooped as he raced into the lead.

Suddenly, Recess, a small brown Labrador

retriever pup, zoomed past the pack. She cheered on her friends as she pulled out in front. "Run fast, mates!"

Wally looked over his shoulder. Spike was catching up to him. "Spike?" Wally woofed in surprise. The chubby bulldog was strong. But who knew he was so fast?

"Ahoy, Wally." Spike's breath came in quick huffs. "I don't love runnin', but Curly said the last one to the finish line gets the teeny steak! I better hurry." Then Spike's paw landed on an icy patch. The big bulldog slipped and slid, and Wally took his chance to zoom past. Spike howled, "Save me a steak, Waaaaaally!"

Wally focused on the finish line. He was more than halfway there. If he could keep up this pace, he was sure to finish in the top five! He ducked his head and ran as fast as he could.

But running was hard work. His legs whined.

His lungs burned. Wally started to slow down. Then he heard Henry whoop, "You can do it, mate!"

At the sound of his best friend's cheer, Wally felt a surge of energy. He sped up enough to catch Recess—and dash past her!

The finish line got closer and closer. Wally could almost smell the steak waiting for him. He glanced back and saw that he was way ahead of

most of his crewmates. With a spring in his step, Wally took another leap forward and then . . .

Huh? For a second, it had seemed like the crate of steak was *moving*! But he must have been imagining it.

With another burst of speed, Wally charged toward the finish line.

Zip! The crate moved again!

The faster Wally ran *toward* the finish line,

the faster it seemed to glide *away* from him. "Avast!" Wally called. Then he realized he was yelling at a crate of steaks. He closed his mouth tight.

That's when Wally saw a flash of something tan hiding behind the crate. Whatever it was had a curly tail, a gold tooth, and a chubby belly. Wally was pretty sure he recognized that belly.

Piggly was playing a prank again. Which meant Puggly couldn't be far behind.

Wally pulled up alongside the crate and spotted the pug twins. They had ropes tied around their chests. The other ends of the ropes were looped around the crate. The crate glided across the snow like a boat.

The pugs were trying to steal the steaks! Wally had to stop them. He took a flying leap and caught his front paws on the very edge of the crate. He scrambled to pull himself inside, just as Piggly and Puggly tugged on their ropes.

The crate jolted forward. Wally tumbled backward into the snow.

Right away, he leaped to his feet again. Wally wasn't going to let two naughty pugs steal the crew's dinner!

And he *really* wanted to win the tryouts.

Wally chased after the pugs and their snow boat. With a mighty howl, he jumped. He landed inside the crate just as it picked up even more speed. A moment later, the pugs jumped in beside him. Wally looked back—all the other puppy pirates had stopped to stare and bark at them.

"Hey, mates!" Henry hollered. "Wait for me!" The boy charged forward and grabbed on. Henry toppled in beside Wally, Piggly, and Puggly as the crate slipped and slid across the snow. Cold air and icy snowflakes stung Wally's nose. The crate whizzed faster and faster . . . and then plunged over the edge of a giant hill!

3

North Pole Racers

Wally howled as the crate barreled down, down, down. Piggly's tongue flapped in the whipping wind like a long pink flag. Puggly's ears fluttered and wiggled as the riders plunged through the snow.

The wind sounded like thunder. Wally's tummy felt bouncy, like when their ship went over big waves. He was excited but also a little nervous!

"In case you were wondering?" Henry yelled.

He wrapped a protective arm around Wally as the crate soared over a bump. "This is the biggest sledding hill I've ever seen!"

Their snow boat raced past icy pine trees and frozen bushes. "*Ar-ar-arrrr-oooo!*" howled Piggly. Her gold tooth glinted in the glow of the setting sun.

Would they ever reach the bottom? The hill felt endless. And then, suddenly, a giant snow pile loomed ahead of them. They were speeding straight toward it. "Watch ooooooooooooout!" Wally shouted.

CRASH. The crate plowed into the heap of fluffy white snow. It toppled over, and the four friends tumbled out. Piggly and Puggly whooped with delight.

Wally was amazed they were all still in one piece. "Woof!" he cheered. "That was fun!"

Puggly shook the snow off her back. "Aye. And our plan worked. We have a whole crate of steaks all to ourselves." She and Piggly giggled and bumped bottoms.

Henry craned his neck, looking up at the top of the hill. *Way* up. "Riding downhill sure was fun. But I'm not looking forward to the climb back *to the top*."

"Well, shiver me timbers." Piggly flopped onto the snow and groaned. "I never thought about that."

"We only planned out the part where we'd steal the crate and eat all the steaks," Puggly pointed out. "We weren't supposed to go flying down a hill!"

"But we *did* slide down," Wally said. "And our whole crew is back up at the top, waiting for their dinner. We better start climbing now, or it will be dark before we get there."

"In case you were wondering, winter days are supposed to be dark at the North Pole," Henry said. "We should get back to the ship. It will be very cold out here in the snow if the sun goes down!"

Puggly whined, "Can't we eat a few steaks first, so the crate will be lighter to pull?"

As soon as Puggly said the word *steaks*, Wally's tummy rumbled. He decided Puggly had a good point. If the crate weighed less, it would be easier to pull up the hill. Wally was about to leap in and take out juicy steaks for everyone. But he stopped when a bunch of strange voices rang out nearby.

"Mush!" one of the voices barked. "All right, let's go! Haw! Haw!"

Wally and the pugs froze. The hair on Piggly's back sprang up as a warning. Wally sniffed the air. Did he smell danger?

Seconds later, a pack of husky pups came racing toward the group. They were running in two lines. It looked like the pups were tied together. Wally and the other puppy pirates sometimes did that during a big storm at sea so no one would fall overboard. But why would dogs be tied together on land?

Henry lifted his hand in greeting. "Ahoy!" His call echoed in the snowy canyon.

The huskies ran toward Wally and his friends. They were moving very quickly! And they were towing a very large snow boat. Wally was sorry to see it had no steaks in it.

Just as the husky crew reached Wally and his friends, one of them cried, "Whoa!" All the dogs stopped.

"Ahoy!" Henry said again. "That's quite a sled you've got there."

Wally wondered what he meant. Were *snow boats* called *sleds*?

"Thank you," said one of the pups at the front of the line. "Welcome to the North Pole, pups. My name is Blizzard, and this is my crew. Are you out on a training run?" Blizzard nosed at the

ropes connecting Piggly and Puggly to the crate full of steaks. "Your tug lines are twisted."

"What's a tug line?" asked Wally.

The team of huskies laughed. Then Blizzard realized that Wally was serious. She barked for silence. "A tug line is the rope that connects your harness to the tow line."

"But what's a tow line?" Wally asked.

"It's what you use to pull your sled," Blizzard answered. "You're not from around here, are you?"

"No, we're from the *Salty Bone*," Wally explained. "That's a pirate ship."

"A ship?" woofed Blizzard. "What are a bunch of sea pups doing out here in the snow?"

"We sailed to the North Pole so we could enter the Great Ice Race. We are going to win the greatest treasure of all!" said Wally.

The pack of huskies howled with laughter again. "I hate to break it to you, pups," Blizzard barked, "but we win the race *every* year. The greatest treasure *belongs* to us. We are the North Pole Racers. Also known as the fastest team in the world."

Piggly and Puggly both took a step forward, growling. "Oh, yeah?" snarled Piggly.

"Yeah," snapped the huskies.

"But everyone knows treasure and pirates go together like . . ." Puggly stopped to think.

"Like salt and water!" Piggly shouted. "Like Henry and Wally! Like me and steak! That treasure will be *ours.*"

Wally stepped between the pugs and the huskies. There was no use arguing. They would just *show* the North Pole Racers how good puppy pirates were at treasure hunting.

It turned out the huskies had the same idea. "How about we show you how fast we are?" Blizzard suggested. "I'm guessing you need to get back up the hill to the docks? We could give you a ride in our sled."

This idea cheered up Piggly and Puggly. Without a moment's thought, both pugs leaped into the wooden sled and got comfortable.

"Oh!" Henry said, climbing in beside them. "Do we get to ride? I've always wanted to lead a racing team!"

The huskies chuckled. "Oh, human," said Blizzard. "No matter how loud you yell, it will be *us* leading *you*."

Wally hopped in beside his friends. The pugs untied themselves from the steak crate, and the huskies tied it to the back of their sleigh. Then they set off running up the hill.

Henry shouted strange words at them: "Mush! Hike!" He turned to Wally and the pugs and explained, "In case you were wondering, those are commands for racing dogs. Mush! Let's go!"

Wally pawed at a pile of blankets. He was getting worried. "No wonder they always win the Great Ice Race," he said. "If they can run this fast dragging a sled, think how fast they will race *without* it!"

Suddenly, a small *yip* rang out from beneath the blankets. A tiny husky nose poked through. The little pup's icy blue eyes peered at Wally

and his friends. "They *won't* race without it," he said softly. Then he cocked his head and asked, "You know the Great Ice Race is a *dogsled* race, right?"

"A *dogsled* race?" Wally barked.

The husky pup nodded. "You can't win the treasure if you don't know how to drive a sled."

The pirate pups didn't know how to drive a sled. They didn't even *have* a sled. Wally and the pugs exchanged nervous looks. Wally was pretty sure they were all thinking the same thing: *Uh-oh.*

Search for a Sled

The huskies raced toward the top of the hill. Wally could tell they were working very hard. Would the pirate crew be able to pull a sled like this through ice and snow? Where would they even *get* a sled before tomorrow's race?

"Thank you for telling us about the race," Wally said to the tiny husky pup. "What's your name?"

"Frosty." The husky shivered in a sudden

gust of wind. He burrowed into his blankets. Soon only his nose and eyes were showing.

"Hi, Frosty. I'm Wally." He introduced Piggly, Puggly, and Henry. Then he asked, "Why are you riding back here in the sled? Shouldn't you be training for the race with the rest of your crew?"

"It's too cold!" Frosty said. "I don't like to be cold. But I love to explore. The pack sometimes lets me ride along in the sled so I won't miss out on any of their adventures."

Before Wally could ask any more questions, the husky team slowed to a stop. Wally was surprised to see that they had already arrived back at the harbor! The North Pole Racers were very fast indeed. He and the *Salty Bone* crew would have some tough competition.

Captain Red Beard and the rest of the puppy pirates raced over as soon as Wally and his friends spilled out of the sled. "About time," the captain barked. "My race was half an hour ago! Where have you been?"

Wally didn't want to get the pugs in trouble with the captain. So he said, "We had a little trouble with, um, a slippery crate, sir."

"Slippery crate?" the captain said.

"It's a long story," Wally said. The pugs both gave him grateful smiles.

"I don't like long stories," the captain grumbled. "Unless I'm the one telling them. So let's get on with our business. Congratulations to Walty, Recess, Leo, Spike, and Wayne. You were the fastest five, so you will join me in the race for the greatest treasure of all."

Wally wagged his tail happily. He couldn't wait to race!

"Who are you?" Red Beard barked, turning to the husky pups. "Why do you have my steaks?

What are you doin' with me crew? Are you spies?"

"These are the North Pole Racers," Wally explained. "They just gave us some very useful information about the Great Ice Race, Captain."

"Useful, eh?" said Captain Red Beard. "What kind of information?"

"Did you know we need a sled if we want to race?" Wally asked.

"Of course I knew that!" barked Red Beard. Quietly, he added, "But remind me, what *is* a sled?"

"That," Wally said, pointing at the husky sled. "It's a kind of snow boat that we have to pull."

"Well, shiver me timbers," Captain Red Beard growled. "Where are we going to get one of those before tomorrow?"

"I know someone who might be able to help you," Frosty said, poking his nose out of the blankets. "If you follow us into town, I can take you to her shop."

Henry hopped into the husky sled, along with Old Salt, a peg-legged Bernese mountain dog. Old Salt was a great sailor and a wise pup, but he didn't do much running these days. The rest of the puppy pirate crew raced after the huskies into town.

When they reached the village, Wally gasped. His eyes widened. There was so much to see! Dozens of colorful buildings framed the edges of a big snowy park. Bright lights and shiny balls hung from all the trees. Puppies wearing cheerful red hats jumped and played in the snow. It was the happiest town Wally had ever visited.

Frosty squirmed out of his blanket in the back of the sled. "Follow me," he told Red Beard and his crew. The little pup led them across the park to a bright red building on a corner of the

town square. A red-and-white sign hung on the door.

"North Pole Adventures?" Henry read. "Fun!"

Henry, Wally, and the crew squeezed inside the shop. The shelves lining the walls were filled with toys and treats. A big open space in the center was covered with warm rugs and cuddly beds. But there were no sleds in sight.

Spike and Humphrey curled up in front of a crackling fire. The pugs sniffed around and found a bowl filled with treat samples. The rest of the crew explored the treasures on the shelves.

Within seconds, all the puppy pirates began barking about things they wanted—especially Captain Red Beard. "This is on my gift list," he said, pointing at a light-up tennis ball. "And this, and this, and this, and this. I want one of everything! 'Tis the season for getting stuff!"

Wally looked around the shop. There were

Frisbees and bouncing balls in every color of the rainbow. Stuffed toys that squeaked, squawked, and sang songs. Bones filled with cheese, peanut butter, and sausage. Ropes and tug toys and chew toys. Wally wondered if he might be able to find Henry the perfect gift. Though there were lots of great things, nothing seemed quite right.

A few minutes after they arrived, a human

woman stepped out from the back of the store. Her gray hair was twisted up into a messy bun that was held in place with a long paintbrush. She was wearing bright green pants, a red-and-white-striped shirt, and tall black work boots. She greeted the group warmly: "Hello! Welcome to the North Pole! Who do we have here?"

"Ahoy," Henry said, stepping forward. "My name is Henry, and these are the puppy pirates."

"Pleased to meet you, Henry. You can call me Mrs. C.," she said with a smile. "Are you pups here for the race?"

"I wish," Henry told her. "But we don't have a sled!"

"That's why I brought them here," Frosty barked. "I thought you might be able to help the puppy pirates get ready for tomorrow's race."

"Aye," barked Captain Red Beard. "We need a sled so we can win the greatest treasure of all!"

"At North Pole Adventures, we like to make sure every pup gets what they want out of their trip to the North Pole," Mrs. C. said. She pointed at a wall covered in pictures. There were puppies skidding across frozen lakes. Puppies pawing up steep mountains. Puppies racing down snowy slopes. And there were puppies pulling sleds. Lots and lots of sleds.

Wally's heart thumped faster. Maybe Mrs. C. *could* help them.

"Let me see what I can do for you," Mrs. C. said, wrapping one strong arm around Henry's shoulders.

She waved for everyone to follow her through a doorway. Wally trotted along, into a garage at the back of the shop. It was huge . . . and empty.

Well, almost empty. In the far corner, there was one sled. It had cracked sides and a broken rail. Wally's hopes fell. This sled didn't look like it could slide very far. Definitely not across the finish line of the Great Ice Race.

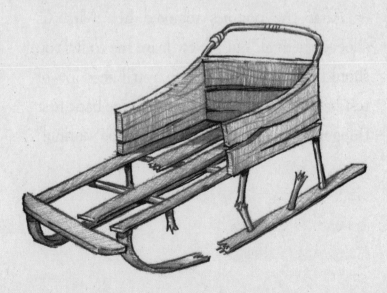

"If I work all night, I think I can fix it," Mrs. C. said. "Then it's all yours."

Captain Red Beard cocked his head. "How much will this cost?" he asked.

"In case you were wondering, we don't have any way to pay you," Henry told Mrs. C.

"Don't worry about that," Mrs. C. said. "I told you, it's my job to give pups a North Pole adventure, and the Great Ice Race is the greatest adventure of all. Besides, as my husband would say, ''Tis the season for giving.'"

After the puppies thanked her, Mrs. C. shooed them all out. "Now leave me to it. You should get back to your ship. You'll need lots of rest before tomorrow's big race. Come back first thing in the morning. Your sled will be waiting!"

5

Learning the Ropes

To thank Frosty for all his help, Wally invited him to spend the night on the *Salty Bone*. The little husky pup was *very* excited. "My pack sleeps outside in the snow," he told Wally. "I hate sleeping on the cold ground! It takes me half the day to warm up again."

"I sleep in a cozy bed," Wally told him. "I can give you a tour of our ship, and then you can bunk with me and Henry for the night."

Wally showed his new friend every nook and

cranny on the *Salty Bone*. He took him to the map room. He showed him how they worked the sails. He even let Frosty peek inside Steak-Eye's kitchen. Frosty *loved* the kitchen, especially when Steak-Eye gave him a bowl of warm stew. After the tour, Frosty curled up in Wally's bed and fell fast asleep. In the morning, he told Wally he'd had his best sleep ever.

During breakfast, Frosty shared stories about life at the North Pole. He told the puppy pirates that his pack spent most of the year training for the Great Ice Race. "Sometimes the team takes trips that last for many days," he said. "That's when I bring extra *extra* blankets."

Wally loved Frosty's stories. But he felt bad that the poor pup was so cold all the time.

Once everyone was full of warm breakfast stew, the puppy pirates followed Frosty back into the village. The sun was just peeking over the horizon as they reached the town square. Mrs. C. was standing beside the simple wooden sled. It looked fixed! In fact, there didn't seem to be a single scratch on it!

"Perfect timing," Mrs. C. said. Today, she was wearing a striped red-and-white snowsuit. "Are you sea pups ready to try out your sled?" She glanced at the sun and added, "You only have a little time to practice before the race starts.

Would you like some help getting set up?"

"Yes, please," Henry said.

"Walty! Spike! Recess! Wayne! Leo!" Captain Red Beard called his race team forward. "It's time for us to show those North Pole Racers what we've got."

Before they could run, the race team had to put on harnesses. This was harder than it looked. There were dozens of straps and hooks on each harness. No one could figure out which

end went where. Henry and Mrs. C. helped,
but it still took forever.

"I'll tell you what's *not* on my Christmas gift
list," Captain Red Beard grumbled. "A harness.
This thing hurts my belly and feels icky-poo on
my fur."

After all six pups had their harnesses on,
Mrs. C. told them they needed to decide what
order they would run in.

"In case you were wondering," Henry blurted

out, "I've read a *lot* of books about dogsledding. If there are six pups racing, we want two lead dogs, two team dogs, and two wheel dogs. The lead dogs will be up front. The team dogs will be in the middle. Wheel dogs are usually the strongest dogs on a crew, and they run right in front of the sled."

Mrs. C. nodded. "That's exactly right, Henry. You know quite a bit for a rookie!"

"I will be the lead dog," Captain Red Beard announced. "Walty, you can race up front with me. Wayne and Spike, you are the wheel dogs. My two Labradors, Leo and Recess, should take the middle."

"Aye, aye, Captain," the pups barked.

Once their team of six was organized, Mrs. C. helped attach their harnesses to something she called rigging. There were ropes that connected the dogs to each other and ropes that connected their team to the sled.

It wasn't long before a small crowd had gathered around the puppy pirate crew. The North Pole Racers and several other dog teams watched the *Salty Bone* racers with great interest. Millie and Stink—a pair of puppy pirates who called themselves the Weirdos—danced and sang pirate shanties to entertain the crowd.

"Now," Mrs. C. said to Henry. "I assume you'll be riding in the sled?"

"For sure!" Henry said.

"Let's go over your commands," Mrs. C. said. "*Gee* is the command for a right turn. *Haw* is what you use to go left. You can start your team by saying *mush* or *hike* or *let's go* or—"

"I'm *bored!*" whined Captain Red Beard. "What's the point of learning all these commands? I'm not letting Walty's human order me around, so I say we just *run*. Ready, me crew? Let's go!"

The captain took off. He only ran a few short steps before coming to a sudden stop.

"*Graaaaw,*" Red Beard choked out, fighting against his own harness. "The rest of ya forgot to run!" He backed up, then barked out, "Hike!"

This time, all six pups began to run. Henry jumped into the sled, hollering, "Mush! Mush! Head straight across the square!" Following his best mate's orders, Wally ran straight ahead.

But after only a few seconds, the pups all caught a whiff of grilled sausages coming from somewhere to their left. "This way!" Red Beard woofed. "*Haw! Haw!*" He turned and ran to the left. Wally felt the tug on his harness and shifted, trying to stay in step with the captain.

Behind them, Henry screamed, "*Gee! Gee!*"

All this shouting caused big problems! Recess went right. Leo went left. Their ropes crossed over each other and quickly tangled. In the back of the line, Wayne stepped on Spike's foot. The chubby bulldog howled, then stopped running altogether.

The ropes attached to the dogs' harnesses tugged and pulled. The sled lurched to a stop. All six pups growled and barked at each other, while Henry shouted from the sled.

Wally looked over and saw the North Pole Racers chuckling and whispering to each other.

Mrs. C. shook her head as she helped untangle the ropes. "Oh, dear," she muttered.

Wally's tail drooped. If they wanted to win, they needed to work together—and fast!

But before they could take another practice run, a loud bell jingled in the center of the square. Packs of dogs raced toward a red line painted on the snow. They all pulled their sleds like pros. Mrs. C. clapped her hands and cried, "Gather round! This year's Great Ice Race is about to begin!"

6

Race Rules

The puppy pirates hobbled toward the starting line. They moved very slowly, trying not to tangle their ropes again.

"Welcome!" Mrs. C. called as soon as all the teams were lined up. She had somehow managed to change out of her snowsuit and was now wearing white pants with a black-and-white-striped top. She had a whistle around her neck and was holding a checkered flag. "Welcome to the Great Ice Race! As I am sure you are aware, the winner of the race will win the greatest treasure of all."

"Gold!" Captain Red Beard guessed, pawing at the ground. "Jewels! Treasure, treasure, treasure, I *want* that treasure! Gimme, gimme, gimme."

Wally scoped out the competition. There were at least twenty teams at the starting line.

One team was made up of giant Saint Bernards, who had small wooden barrels tied around their necks. They looked *very* tough.

A group of Dalmatians pulled a bright red sled that looked like a fire truck. A crew of sleek greyhounds wore matching harnesses and blue booties. The North Pole Racers all wore pointed red hats with soft white trim.

Henry called the Weirdos over. Millie and Stink *loved* dressing up in costumes. Millie wore fluffy black earmuffs. Stink had a pirate hat almost as big as he was. Henry whispered to them, "Mates, I should be wearing something pirate-y! Do you think I could borrow your hat, Stink?"

"Aye!" Stink woofed.

Henry stuck the hat on his head. "Perfect," he said. Wally thought he looked even more pirate-y than usual.

The other teams had one thing in common: they were all pulling a beautiful sleigh. Some were covered in jewels. Others were decorated with painted designs or wooden carvings. One sleigh was sparkling silver and full of flashing lights and dials—it looked ready to slide into space! Only the puppy pirates had a sled made out of plain brown wood.

Very simple.

Very boring.

"Nice sled, pirate pups," one of the North Pole Racers said, smirking.

Blizzard shushed him. "Don't be a bad sport, Dasher," she scolded. "That's not the spirit of this competition."

"I don't want to pull the worst sled," Captain Red Beard muttered. "I only like being the best!"

"It doesn't matter what our sled looks like," Wally reminded the captain. "The only thing that matters is how fast it goes."

The puppies paid close attention as Mrs. C. explained the rules. "The beginning of the race is simple. Speed and strength will be important. You will follow Gumdrop Trail out of the village, race through Candy Cane Forest, and then cross the bridge over Gingerbread River."

Gumdrop Trail? Wally thought, giggling. *Candy Cane Forest? Gingerbread River?* The North Pole sounded delicious!

Mrs. C. went on, "If any of you don't know

the way, just follow the North Pole Racers—they know this route better than anyone. But when you reach Cotton Candy Caves, each team will be on its own. From there, you will need to use your noodles if you want to win the greatest treasure of all."

"Aww, we don't *have* any noodles," Captain Red Beard whined. "I have *steak,* I have *stew,* but I don't have noodles. No curly noodles, no straight noodles, no cheesy noodles. No noodles at all!"

"In case you were wondering," Henry whispered to Wally and the other pups, "*noodle* is a silly word for *brain.*"

"Each team will get a map," Mrs. C. said. She handed out pieces of parchment. "I have set up three checkpoints along the course. At each checkpoint, your team will get a riddle. Solve the riddle, and you will get the next part of your map. The first team to reach the finish line will earn a special key—"

"Is it a gold key?" Captain Red Beard barked out. Curly shushed him.

Mrs. C. went on, "This special key will unlock the treasure."

Captain Red Beard howled with joy. "A map?" he woofed. "Riddles? No one is better at map reading and riddle solving than my puppy pirates!" He called the pugs over. "Piggly, Puggly—you don't run fast, but you are very good at solving riddles. You will ride in our sled and help out."

The pugs cheered. They *loved* being part of

the action. Wally also had a feeling they wanted to snack on candy canes, gumdrops, and cotton candy along the way!

"Maybe I could also ride along in your sled during the race?" Frosty asked. He stepped forward shyly. "In case you need some help figuring out how your ropes and the sled work?"

Captain Red Beard glared at the little husky pup. "Shouldn't you ride with your own team?"

Frosty shook his head. "They don't need me. But I might be helpful to you." He wagged his tail eagerly. "It would be nice to feel useful."

"Captain," Wally said, "maybe we should bring him along. Frosty knows a lot about dog-sledding."

"Fine," Red Beard huffed. "But I am not sharing the treasure."

Frosty climbed into the sled. He curled up between Piggly and Puggly, and then sighed happily. "It's a lot cozier when you have friends in the sled!" he said.

Mrs. C. waved her checkered flag. "Pups, are you ready?"

All the dogs tensed, prepared for action. Wally took a deep breath.

"Get set!" Mrs. C. hollered.

Wally got set. Henry whooped.

"And . . . GO!"

7

Dashing Through the Snow

The flag swooped down, and the dogs took off! Barking and yipping, teams of six raced across the town square. The huskies took the lead right away. Sled after sled slid out of the village and into the snowy world beyond.

The rest of the *Salty Bone* crew barked and cheered from the sidelines. Millie and Stink rang little sleigh bells and sang merrily.

"*Arr-arrrr-oooo!*" Curly yipped. "Stay strong, mates!"

"*Yo-ho-haroo!*" woofed Old Salt.

Henry waved a pirate flag at the crowd.

Pulling the sled through snow was easier than Wally had feared. Especially without Henry and Captain Red Beard yelling opposite commands. They weren't anywhere close to the lead, but at least they weren't tangled up in their own ropes. And because their sled was simple and plain, it was surely much lighter to pull than some of the other teams' fancy sleighs!

The snow turned everything white. But Wally could still see the North Pole Racers' red hats bobbing in the distance. They reminded Wally of a lighthouse, guiding the way.

Gumdrop Trail led them to a red-and-white forest. The trees looked a whole lot like ... candy canes? Wally couldn't believe it. "That must be Candy Cane Forest," Henry said. He ran one finger along the map, tracing their route.

"Can we stop for a taste?" Piggly begged.

"No," Captain Red Beard told her. "We don't stop until I have my treasure."

Piggly and Puggly both sighed. "What about what *we* want?" Puggly whined. "Don't our wishes count?" With the mention of wishes, Wally remembered he hadn't yet found the perfect gift for Henry. Maybe his best mate would like a giant candy cane?

At the edge of Candy Cane Forest, Mrs. C. popped up out of nowhere. She was wearing a red beret. The little red hat made Mrs. C. look like she was a part of the forest. She held a camera in front of her face and yelled, "Say cheese!"

"Cheese?" Puggly woofed. "Where? I love cheese!"

The North Pole Racers were way out in the lead, and getting farther ahead every minute. It seemed as if they were flying across the snow— their feet hardly touched down between steps! The huge, strong Saint Bernards were right behind them. The Dalmatians and their fire-truck sleigh were running ahead of the puppy pirates, and the greyhounds were close at their heels. So far, it was a very close race!

Wally and his team chased after the leaders. Though they were tired, the *Salty Bone* crew would never give up. They ran as fast as they could, weaving through stalks of red-and-white candy canes. Henry called, "Mush! Mush!" and his friends' paws pounded against the snow. By the time they reached the far side of Candy Cane Forest, the puppy pirates were in fourth place!

Families of gingerbread men, women, and children cheered for the dogsled teams as they dashed across the bridge over Gingerbread River. "Ahoy!" Henry shouted, waving his flag.

On the other side of the river, a ridge of blue and pink mountains loomed ahead of them. Henry called out, "Whoa!" On his command,

the puppy pirate team skidded to a stop. When they did, the sleek greyhounds and a team of stylish standard poodles zipped past them.

Henry pointed at the horizon. "Look!"

"What are ya doing?" Captain Red Beard said, tugging at his harness. "This is a *race*. There's no time to stop and enjoy the scenery."

Henry waved Mrs. C.'s map in the air. "Mates, look at the map! Cotton Candy Caves should be inside those big blue and pink lumps over there." Henry pointed east, in a slightly different direction than the poodles and greyhounds were heading.

"Who is leading this team?" Captain Red Beard demanded. "I get to read the map. I get to decide which way we go! I am the captain."

Frosty poked his head out of the sled and said, "But, sir, I think the boy is right. To get to Mrs. C.'s first checkpoint, we need to go east around Cotton Candy Caves and cross the Snow Cone Glaciers."

Piggly glanced at the map. "It's true."

Red Beard pawed at the ground. "What is this hoodly-toodly nonsense? Let me see the map. I don't believe you."

Red Beard studied the parchment. Finally, he said, "We need to go that way—east around Cotton Candy Caves."

"But that's exactly . . . ," Wally began. He was about to point out that Henry, Frosty, and Piggly had said the same thing. But he knew the captain wouldn't want to hear it.

Then Wally thought of something Captain Red Beard *would* want to hear. "Captain," he barked. "We have something special that none of the other teams have."

"What is it?" Captain Red Beard asked. "It better not be fleas."

Wally shook his head. "We have *helpers* riding in our sled. None of the other teams have anyone in their sleigh. If we leave the map reading to Henry, Frosty, and the pugs, we won't have to stop running to study the map!"

"Hmmm," Captain Red Beard said, cocking his head. "Little Walty, something you just said gave me an idea." He howled, "From now on, the human, Frosty, and our two pugs will be in charge of reading the map and directing our sled. The race team and I will focus on running."

The captain stomped his paw in the snow. "Now onward, racers—to Cotton Candy Caves!"

8

Winter Riddle

The puppy pirates set off running across the snowy plain. The dogsled teams had spread out after Candy Cane Forest, so now the puppy pirates had no other teams to follow. Red Beard's crew was on its own.

As they raced toward Cotton Candy Caves, the snow came down harder. Once, Wally thought he spotted the North Pole Racers' red hats again in the distance. But he wasn't sure. It was hard to see much of *anything* while the sky was full of swirling snowflakes.

Finally, they reached Cotton Candy Caves. Wally wished they had time to explore. What kind of treasures might be hidden inside such colorful caves? He imagined jewels made of sugar, rocks made of peanut butter, and walls covered in tasty rawhide.

But cave exploring would have to wait for another day. Today, they were on a quest for a different kind of treasure—the *greatest* treasure of all. There was no time to stop and smell the treats. Instead, the team turned east to go around the pink and blue mountains and shot out onto the rainbow-colored Snow Cone Glaciers.

Henry yelled commands, guiding the crew over giant cracks in the ice. Sometimes the puppy pirates had to stop, back up, and steer around icy pools. Playful seals and honking

narwhals poked their heads out of the water and cheered them on.

Wally was beginning to feel tired. The sled felt heavier with each step he took. Spike had little ice balls stuck between his paw pads. Wayne was having trouble keeping his harness in place. The pugs moaned that they were *starving*.

Just when Wally thought they should stop for a rest, he spotted a huge red-and-green flag flapping ahead of them. The flag was planted at the base of an icy mountain. "In case you were wondering?" Henry cried. "I think we found the first checkpoint, mates!"

The sounds of barking and cheering got louder as they drew closer to the mountain. Dozens of puppies had taken a shortcut to the first checkpoint so they could cheer the racers on. As the puppy pirates' team ran toward the flag, Millie and Stink burst into song.

"Splashing through the snow," the two Weirdos sang, "in a six-dog pirate sleigh, o'er the ice they go, running all the way—*yo-ho-ho!*"

"Whoa!" Henry cried. "Halt!" The puppy pirates came to a stop under the giant flag. Little elf pups surrounded the crew. The small, fluffy white dogs were wearing tiny red-and-green-striped hats decorated with jingling bells. They offered each of the race pups dishes of hot meat stew and bowls of cold water.

While he gobbled up his snack, Wally

searched the crowd for Mrs. C. Before they could collect the next section of their map, they needed to solve her riddle. But where was she? And where were the other teams?

A moment later, a loud *Yoo-hoo!* rang out from above. Wally and the other pups looked up to see Mrs. C. sliding down a rope off the edge of the icy mountain. She was wearing climbing gear and gloves. Her harness reminded Wally of the one he had to wear to pull their sled.

"Welcome," Mrs. C. said, landing on the ground with a soft thump. "Congratulations on making it to the first checkpoint. You are the third team to arrive."

"Third?" Recess yipped with glee. "We're in third place?"

Mrs. C. added, "The North Pole Racers and the Saint Bernards are just ahead of you."

"I hate third place," grumbled Captain Red Beard.

"Are you ready for your riddle?" Mrs. C. smiled at Wally and his mates. "Remember, no hints from the crowd. Only racers on your sled can guess the answer. Here goes:

> "When it's cold outside,
> everyone loves
> these little white stars
> that sprinkle from above.
> What are they?"

Captain Red Beard woofed happily. "Stars!" he said. "Twinkling stars! That's easy. I am very good at solving riddles."

"That might be it, sir," Piggly began. "But

I'm pretty sure she said *sprinkle,* not *twinkle*—"

"SNOW!" Henry hollered. "I think the answer is snow."

"Very good," Mrs. C. said, grinning. She handed Henry a map. "Good luck on the second leg of your race. I'll see you next at the Ancient Licorice Tree!"

9

The Final Stretch

As the puppy pirate crew raced away from Mrs. C., Wally heard the crowd let out a cheer. He glanced back. The Dalmatian team had just pulled into the checkpoint. "Run, run," Captain Red Beard growled. "We can't let anyone catch us!"

Luckily, the warm stew had given everyone on the team energy. Wally, the captain, Recess, Leo, Spike, and Wayne all ran as fast as their legs would allow. If they caught up to the North

Pole Racers and the Saint Bernards, they could slide into first place!

Wally heard Henry, Frosty, and the pugs trying to map out the fastest route to the next checkpoint. "I think we should take Sugar Plum Meadow to Marshmallow Bog," Frosty told the others. "It's the shortest path."

"Haw!" Henry yelled. The pups turned to the left. "To Sugar Plum Meadow!" As they set off at a gallop, Wally glanced to his right. In the distance, he could see that the Saint Bernards had chosen a different route. Wally was sure that Frosty knew the best route and felt lucky they had the little husky on their crew!

When the *Salty Bone* racers reached a purple-snow-covered meadow, Frosty called out friendly greetings to a group of Sugar Plum Fairies who had come to watch the race. The fairies waved their wands in reply. A second later, a pile of

treats appeared in the back of their sled! Piggly and Puggly gobbled them down.

The team raced on through Marshmallow Bog. The *Salty Bone* sled was making good time. Wally spotted the North Pole Racers not far ahead. He was about to alert his teammates when, suddenly, their sled lurched to a stop. "Eh?" Captain Red Beard said, glancing over his shoulder. "Why did you all quit runnin'?"

Frosty and Henry hopped out of the sled to see what had happened. "One of our sled rails is stuck in the bog," Frosty said, shivering like crazy.

Piggly and Puggly climbed out of the sleigh. The two pugs sniffed at the sticky goop on the ground. Piggly took a tiny taste. Puggly took a bigger bite. "This is the yummiest bog on earth," she announced. "Tastes like marshmallow and peanut butter and honey, all mixed up in one cold, delicious stew. It might take a while, but Piggly and I could *lick* our sled free."

"Ugh," Henry groaned. "We need some help. This is a sticky mess!"

"I have an idea," Frosty said. He howled, and a moment later a group of furry creatures came lumbering across the bog. It was a pack of little polar bear cubs! They surrounded the sled, then stuck out their tongues and . . . *licked*.

"Told you so!" Puggly shouted. She and Piggly joined in the fun. It was hard work. Deliciously hard.

Within minutes, the sled was clean, and the puppy pirates were back in action.

"Thanks for your help!" Frosty cried out to the little bear cubs as the pups' sled zoomed away.

"There's the flag," Henry called not long after. He pointed to a red-and-green flag hanging from the tallest branches of a giant black licorice tree. "And there are the North Pole Racers!" Sure enough, just as the puppy pirates pulled into the second checkpoint, the husky team dashed away.

"We're getting closer to first place!" Recess woofed.

As soon as the pups had come to a complete stop, Mrs. C. parachuted out of the sky. Wally couldn't figure out how she had beaten them to the checkpoint. He was starting to think she was as magical as the rest of the North Pole.

"Congratulations on making it to the second

checkpoint," she said. "You are the second team to arrive. Are you ready for your next riddle?"

"Aye!" the puppy pirates barked.

"Okay, here you go," Mrs. C. said. She pulled off a huge pair of goggles and winked.

"I bite but have no teeth.
What am I?"

"A toothless dog?" Captain Red Beard guessed. "The Sea Slug!"

"Bite . . . ," Piggly repeated. "No teeth . . . hmmm, this is a hard one. An eel? A whale?"

Puggly moaned, "It's hard to think straight when your belly's full of marshmallow."

"Frost!" Wally cried all of a sudden. "The cold bites at your paws and fur, but it doesn't have teeth. Is that right?"

Henry's eyes grew wide as he glanced at Mrs. C. "Is it frost?"

"Spot-on, mateys," Mrs. C. said. She handed

Henry the last section of the map, and the puppy pirates took off again. They ran as fast as they could while Henry called out commands.

Breathing hard, the puppy pirate team raced toward the final checkpoint. As they burst out from the other side of Candy Cane Forest, Wally glanced to his left. That's when he saw the North Pole Racers—only a few leaps ahead of them! "We can do this," he barked to his teammates. "We can *win!*"

"Mush!" Henry yelled. "Almost there!"

The racecourse had led the teams in a big circle. Mrs. C.'s final checkpoint was just ahead, and Gumdrop Trail was off to their right. A red-and-green flag waved high in the sky. Crowds of puppies were gathered, cheering and hollering. Wally spotted Old Salt, Curly, the Weirdos, and the rest of the crew rooting for them.

"Our treasure's waiting for us," Captain Red Beard said, panting. "Mush! Mush!"

The puppy pirates sprinted. But every time they drew closer to the husky team, the North Pole Racers shot ahead.

The huskies pulled into the final checkpoint, with the puppy pirates right behind. The crowd went wild. Wally glanced over his shoulder, but he couldn't see any other teams. Their sled might have been simple and plain, but it had served them well! Now the race was down to just two teams. Only one could win.

But which one would it be?

10

The North Pole

"Welcome," Mrs. C. said, cross-country skiing into the final checkpoint. She had magically changed outfits *again*. Now she was wearing a snazzy ski-racing suit and a fluffy hat.

"Congratulations on reaching the final checkpoint," Mrs. C. announced. "You are the first two teams to arrive. The Great Ice Race will come down to my last riddle. Whoever solves it first will get a thirty-second head start for the final stretch of the race."

The puppy pirates and the North Pole Racers eyed each other. Both teams wanted to win. "Where is the finish line?" Henry asked, scanning the horizon.

"Right over there," Mrs. C. said. She pointed across the snowy landscape. "You'll know you have made it to the end when you see the North Pole."

"In case you were wondering?" Henry said, laughing. "There isn't an actual *pole* at the North Pole."

"Is that so?" Mrs. C. said, smiling. She waved her hand. When she did, the wind picked up. Snow swirled and twirled around them in the air. Moments later, a huge red-and-white-striped pole appeared in the distance. Wally was sure it hadn't been there before. "Sometimes you just have to believe. Now, are you ready?" Mrs. C. asked. "Here is your final riddle:

"It has a golden head,
it has a golden tail,
but it has no body.
What is it?"

Both teams began shouting out answers. "A phoenix!" cried Blizzard.

"A yellow Labrador retriever wearing a life jacket!" hollered Captain Red Beard.

Piggly and Puggly put their heads together, whispering. Wally thought hard.

Captain Red Beard stomped his foot and whined, "Come on, pups. I want me gold coins!

I want me riches. I want me presents!"

The husky team all gave him funny looks. "Gold coins?" one of them muttered. "What is he barking about?"

"Wait a second," Henry said, his eyes growing wide. "I think—"

"That's it!" Piggly yipped at her sister.

At the same time, Piggly and Henry shouted, "A GOLD COIN!"

Mrs. C. nodded. "Gold head, gold tail, but no body. The answer is a gold coin, indeed."

"We win!" Captain Red Beard barked. "We win, we win, we win!"

"Thirty-second head start for the puppy pirates!" Mrs. C. hollered. "Ready, set, *goooooo*!"

Henry leaped into the sled, shouting, "Let's go, mates! Mush!"

The puppy pirate crew set off at a run. Thirty seconds was a big head start, but the huskies were *fast*.

The two teams raced through the snow along Gumdrop Trail, toward the red-and-white-striped pole. Wally ran faster than he had ever run before. His heart pounded. His paws plowed through the snow. But no matter how fast the puppy pirates ran, the huskies ran faster. Soon the two teams were neck and neck, nose and nose. Wally and Captain Red Beard leaped across the finish line just as Mrs. C. appeared, waving her flag.

"It's a TIE!" Mrs. C. cried. She snapped a picture of the two winning teams. "Congratulations to the puppy pirates and the North Pole Racers! We've never had a tie before. How fun!"

Wally liked the idea of a tie. The puppy pirates were the fastest riddle solvers, and the huskies were the fastest runners. Maybe this meant they could share the treasure.

Then he remembered how much Captain Red Beard hated to share.

"It's *not* fun," the captain yelped. "It's not *fair*."

"This is *our* treasure," the huskies all howled.

Mrs. C. held up her hands for silence. "Enough yapping," she said. "There is no reason you can't all enjoy the treasure."

"Noooo!" Red Beard wailed. He dropped his head into his paws.

Old Salt, Curly, Steak-Eye, Einstein, and the other puppy pirates gathered around them, barking out congratulations. But Captain Red Beard was too busy moaning. "Treasure is *not* for sharing! Every sailor worth his salt knows that!" He glanced around, then scratched his reddish beard. "Where *is* the treasure, anyway?"

Mrs. C. waved her hand, and the red-and-white-striped pole began to rise up, up, up out of the snow. All the pups backed away as the snow under their paws shook and shuddered. The pole stretched taller and taller. All of a sudden, the roof of some kind of *house* burst out of the snow.

"Whoa," Henry said, his mouth hanging open. Wally stood beside his best mate, watching in wonder as a huge green building grew out of the ground.

Frosty nudged Wally. "I still remember the first time I got to see Santa's workshop. It's really something, isn't it?"

"Did you say . . . um . . . *Santa*?" Wally yelped.

"Welcome to my husband's home away from home," Mrs. C. said. She opened a huge door and invited them all inside. "Welcome to Santa's workshop."

11

The Greatest Treasure of All

"Oh, man," Henry said. He knocked his palm against his forehead. "*C* stands for *Claus*, doesn't it? You're Mrs. *Claus*?"

Mrs. C. laughed. "That's a fact. But I always go by Mrs. C. Too much fame in the family name for my taste. Santa and I, we have very different interests. He loves making toys . . . and eating cookies. His whole year is built around one wonderful, magical night. Me, I prefer a little more action and adventure *every* day."

The puppy pirates followed Mrs. Claus and the North Pole Racers into a giant room that was *stuffed* with goodies. The pups from the *Salty Bone* sniffed in corners and poked their noses onto shelves. Mrs. Claus gave them time to explore every inch of the workshop.

More little elf pups bustled around them, hard at work building new toys, wrapping presents, and baking treats.

"This is the best treasure *ever!*" Captain Red Beard barked, gazing around the workshop. "Toys, games, snacks, stuffed ducks . . . every single thing on my list is inside this workshop!"

Wally barked excitedly. Maybe he would finally find the perfect gift for Henry inside Santa's workshop. He nosed through piles of toys and treats, but nothing inside the shop seemed *perfect* enough.

Mrs. Claus clapped for attention. "Shall we get to the treasure, then?"

"Isn't *this* the treasure?" Henry asked.

Mrs. Claus laughed. "Oh, dear me, no. The real treasure is in there." She pointed to a huge door. Then she held up a gold key. "Who wants to do the honors?"

Captain Red Beard and Blizzard both raced forward. They shoved and wrestled, trying to get to the key first. Finally, the two teams' captains fell to the ground in a tangle of legs and paws.

Shaking her head, Mrs. Claus slipped the key into the lock and turned it. Then she looked at Frosty. "You, pup, went out of your way to help our visitors take part in the race today. So I will let *you* do the honors. You have truly embraced the spirit of this season. Please, friend, show us the treasure."

Frosty stepped forward. He nudged the door open with his nose. On the other side was a huge golden—

"Sleigh!" Henry cried. "It's Santa's sleigh! But . . . I always thought *reindeer* pulled Santa's sleigh?"

"Ho ho ho," Mrs. Claus chuckled. "Everybody knows there's no sled team like a dogsled team!"

The pups raced inside and crowded around the giant golden sled. Captain Red Beard sniffed it. He pawed at it. He tried to dig under it. "Where is the treasure? The gold coins and jewels and such?"

"The greatest treasure of all," Mrs. Claus told everyone, "is having the chance to pull Santa's gifts in this sleigh. You get to help Santa share the joy of this season. What could be better than the gift of giving?"

"This is hoodly-toodly nonsense!" Captain Red Beard wailed. "I am not giving away this treasure. It's *mine*! This season is about *getting*, not *sharing*."

Wally didn't know what to think. Giving sounded like a lot of fun. On the other hand, so did treasure.

Old Salt rapped his peg leg on the floor to get the captain's attention. "Listen here, Captain," he said quietly. "I think you might want to pay attention to what Mrs. Claus is sayin'."

"She said we won a gold sleigh," the captain whined. "But we don't get to keep it!"

Old Salt cleared his throat. "I think what she's actually telling us is that the greatest gift of all is having the chance to share joy with others."

"He's right," Frosty woofed. "I loved helping your crew in the race today, even though it was cold!"

"Remember how much fun it was to help the Weirdos fix up their old ghost ship?" Spike barked. "That was a good day."

"One of my best days ever was pirate school. I loved helping the rest of the crew learn how to read maps," Einstein said quietly.

Wally thought about it. How had Mrs. Claus put it . . . that giving was a gift? Wally realized this was true. That's why he wanted to find the right gift for Henry. Nothing made Wally happier than making his friends happy. That was number one on his wish list. "Giving really is the best gift," he barked. "Maybe we should try this."

Old Salt said, "What do you say, Captain?

I bet we can be the best givers the North Pole has ever seen."

"Aye!" Captain Red Beard woofed. "I *will* be the best. It's time for us to do a little more splashing through the snow!"

But before Red Beard could squeeze into one of the harnesses at the front of the sleigh, Blizzard barked, "Hold up. Our teams *tied* for first. That means we get to pull the sleigh, too."

"Fine," Captain Red Beard said. He didn't look happy. "But I'm in charge."

"No ho ho!" Blizzard laughed. "*I* am in charge."

The two pups growled at each other. Captain Red Beard barked, "Puppy pirates, line up. Let's take the front."

Blizzard howled, "North Pole Racers, line up. *We* will take the front."

There was a mad dash for the harnesses.

Wally was poked and jostled as he wiggled into his harness. He had just slipped his shoulders through when Captain Red Beard called, "Gee!"

At the same moment, Blizzard barked, "Haw!"

The puppy pirates ran right.

The North Pole Racers ran left.

The sled squeaked and creaked. Mrs. Claus shouted, "Be careful! You need to work together. This sleigh is centuries old. We have to treat it with respect or it will—" Mrs. Claus went silent as a loud *CRRRRACK* split the air. Everyone stopped, but it was too late. Mrs. Claus sighed as the sled split in two. "Or it will break."

12

Sailing Through
the Snow

The puppies all froze. They stared at the golden sleigh. A giant crack sliced straight down the middle. Was Christmas *ruined*?

Wally had been pulling to the right, as hard as he could. He felt like this was partly his fault. "I'm sorry!" Wally woofed.

"No, I'm sorry!" the husky named Dasher barked back.

"We're sorry!" Piggly and Puggly yipped together.

Soon all the puppy pirates and the North Pole Racers were apologizing to each other—and to Mrs. Claus. Even Captain Red Beard dipped his nose in his paws. "I'm usually the best at everything," he told Blizzard quietly. "But maybe I'm not the *best* at sharing."

"It was my fault, too," Blizzard told him.

"You're right about that!" Captain Red Beard barked. But he barked it nicely. "And you were also right that a tie means we both won. Your team ran a good race."

"Exactly as good as your team!" Blizzard said.

"In case you were wondering, Santa can't deliver his presents without his sleigh!" Henry said. "What do we do?"

Mrs. Claus shook her head sadly. "I don't know. And Christmas starts *tonight*."

"Can we fix it?" Wally asked. Just as he said that, the sleigh let out another loud *CRRRRACK*. Everyone jumped out of the way as the enormous sled split into four parts. Gifts spilled out, all over the ground.

"We have millions of presents to deliver," Mrs. Claus said. "And no way to deliver them."

"Will Christmas be canceled?" Frosty asked, his head hanging low. The other dogs whined and moaned.

"Canceled?" Red Beard howled. "*Noooooo!*"

"Maybe we could use a different sleigh?" Wally suggested.

"Every team that raced today was pulling a sled," Henry pointed out. "Couldn't Santa use one of those instead?"

"Hmmm." Mrs. Claus frowned. "None of them are big enough. Even if we used all the sleds in the whole village, we still wouldn't have enough room for all these gifts. If I had more time, I could fix Santa's sleigh. But with only one hour until sunset, it's not possible."

"Only one hour till sunset?" Puggly yelped. "No wonder my stomach is grumbling. It's dinnertime!"

At that, Piggly's tummy let out a loud rumble. "I sure could use one of Steak-Eye's steaks right about now," she said. "A pup can't live on marshmallows and peanut butter."

Wally laughed. Even when things were at

their worst, the pugs never stopped thinking about food. Wally was hungry, too. He imagined Steak-Eye's big crates full of steak. Then he suddenly got an idea. "Maybe we have more sleds than we think," he told the others.

"What are you yapping about, little Walty?" Captain Red Beard asked. "Are you hiding sleds?"

"Remember when the pugs turned our steak crate into a sled yesterday?" Wally said, glancing at Piggly and Puggly. "Of course, that wasn't a *real* sleigh—but it worked like one. I bet we could find other things we could turn into sleds for the night. They don't have to be fancy— they just have to do the job."

"I have an idea!" Henry broke in. "Maybe we could use the dinghies from the *Salty Bone* as extra sleighs!" Wally woofed his approval. The little wooden boats that hung off the side of their ship would make *perfect* sleighs!

Mrs. Claus looked hopeful. "It's certainly worth a try," she said.

"But who gets to pull the sleds?" Captain Red Beard asked. "Who gets the treasure?"

Frosty said, "Maybe this year, it's time for the village to start a new tradition. Instead of just the winners getting to deliver presents, *every* pup who wants to join in can pull a sleigh."

"We need all the help we can get," agreed Old Salt.

"Hear, hear!" everyone barked.

For the next hour, the whole village worked together to turn as many things as possible into sleds. Everyone then helped the pups load gifts into hundreds of different sleds. Mrs. Claus took pictures and helped with sled repairs.

The puppies had made sleds out of boxes, food crates, and large Frisbees. Some of these could fit only one or two gifts, but they were light enough that even little pups like Einstein, Curly, and the pugs could pull them. All the Great Ice Race teams loaded their sleds high.

The rest of the *Salty Bone* crew harnessed themselves up to the ship's dinghies. Even though they didn't *look* like sleds, the little boats held lots of gifts. And they slid smoothly over the snow and ice when there was a team of eager pups pulling them!

As the last gifts were loaded, Wally searched for Frosty in the crowd. He found the little husky cuddled up in Mrs. Claus's arms. Frosty was shivering in the biting-cold night air.

"Aren't you coming, Frosty?" Wally asked. He didn't want his friend to miss out.

"Not this time," Frosty told him. His little nose and eyes were the only things sticking out of Mrs. Claus's thick winter parka. "It's too cold tonight."

Mrs. Claus winked at Wally. Then she pulled a special Frosty-sized parka out of her pocket.

"For me?" Frosty said, eyes wide.

"Merry Christmas, Frosty." She slipped the parka over Frosty's pointed ears and zipped it tight against his belly. She wrapped his feet in booties and tucked a warm water bottle into a special pocket on the back of the jacket. "The cold isn't going to keep you from going on this adventure, little pup," she said with a smile. Then she carried Frosty over to the largest sleigh and plopped him onto the seat beside Henry.

"Did you hear that?" Henry asked. He tilted his head, like he was listening to something in the distance.

Wally's ears pricked up. If he listened hard, he could hear bells jingling. The sound was coming from all around them. And it was getting louder.

"There you are!" Mrs. Claus's face lit up with a grin. "I was afraid you would miss it!"

Wally wondered who she was talking to. And then—

"Ho ho ho!" The air shook with a booming laugh. A large human stepped out into the night. The man was wearing a big red hat and stroking his fluffy white beard. He chuckled and said, "*Miss* Christmas? Never!"

"Santa!" the puppies cried. They bounced up and down, waving their tails.

"I hear you pups saved Christmas," Santa said, reaching down to scratch the dogs behind their ears. The puppies all glowed with pride. "Now whose sleigh do I ride in?"

Blizzard cleared her throat. "If you ask me—"

Captain Red Beard barked loudly over her. "I know the answer to this one, Santa!"

Wally watched the two captains nervously. What would Santa think if they started fighting all over again?

"You should ride with the North Pole Racers," Captain Red Beard said. "After all, I hear they're the best sled dogs in the world." He winked at Blizzard. "And Santa deserves the best."

Santa patted Captain Red Beard on the head. He ruffled Wally's fur. Then he climbed into the huskies' sled. "Well, what are we waiting for? Let's get on with the giving!"

Mrs. Claus waved her hand through the air. Sparkling snowflakes swirled all around them. Wally thought he must be imagining it, but for a moment it almost felt as if his feet left the ground. The snug harness around his belly suddenly felt loose and comfortable. And for some reason, the dinghy now felt weightless, even under the weight of hundreds of presents.

Bells jingled from every corner of the village. The time had finally come. Santa bellowed, "Ho ho ho!" and all the dogs set off at a run. Wally raced through the twinkling snow, howling with joy. This was going to be a night none of them would ever forget.

13

Frosty's New Adventure

The next morning, after all the gifts had been delivered, Mrs. Claus invited the pups back to North Pole Adventures. She brought out platters filled with warm sausages and peanut butter treats. Henry sipped a mug of hot chocolate and then played a few songs on his fiddle. All the puppies curled up in front of a crackling fire to rest after a long night of work. In the far corner of the shop, Santa snoozed in a rocking chair.

As soon as Wally finished his breakfast,

Mrs. Claus called him over. "I have something for you," she said. Quietly, she led him into the garage at the back of the shop. She handed him a wrapped package.

"What is it?" Wally asked. He nosed the package open, and dozens of pictures fell out onto the floor. There were pictures of Wally and Henry and their Great Ice Race team. There were pictures of the puppy pirate crew cheering them on. There was even a picture of Frosty. Wally poked through the whole batch. He stopped at a picture of him and Henry, standing side by side in front of a dinghy filled with gifts.

"These are for you to do with as you wish," Mrs. Claus said, smiling.

As soon as she said it, Wally knew *exactly* what he wanted to give Henry for a gift. It wasn't big, it wasn't shiny—but it was perfect. He would make Henry a memory book of their adventure at the North Pole. That way, his best mate would never forget their fun time there.

Mrs. Claus smiled and nodded, even though Wally hadn't said anything. "In case you were wondering, parchment and glue are on the bottom shelf, next to the paint."

Wally got to work. In no time he had a photo book he couldn't wait to share with his friend. He even dipped his paw in red paint and pressed it onto the cover. That way, Henry would know who it was from!

When Wally returned to the front of the shop, his mates from the *Salty Bone* were giving each other gifts. Humphrey had found a blanket for Spike that was just like the one he used—only much bigger. Puggly gave the Weirdos matching elf suits. Santa gave Captain Red Beard a huge box filled with every single thing on his Christmas gift list.

Red Beard eyed the gifts greedily . . . then,

one by one, he passed them out to his crew.

"This stuffed duck is for you," he said to Curly.

"An old shoe suits you," he told Old Salt.

"This tasty bone for you . . . this bag o' jewels for you . . ." This went on until all the gifts were gone. "Givin' gifts is almost as good as gettin' 'em. *Almost*."

Frosty got up from his place beside the fire. "We have a gift for you, our pirate friends," he said. "A present from the North Pole Racers."

Captain Red Beard's tail wagged. "Oh, another present for me? I'll open it!" He tore open the wrapping paper. A pile of tangled ropes spilled out onto the floor.

"We got you your own harnesses and tow lines,"

Frosty said, bouncing up and down with excitement. "If you ever want to rig up a sleigh, you have all the stuff your crew will need to pull it. Maybe you could try pulling some kind of sled through the sand sometime!"

While Captain Red Beard tried on the new gear, the puppy pirates went around thanking the huskies. When Wally got to Frosty, the little pup said, "I was wondering something, Wally."

Wally cocked his head. "What?"

"Do you think Captain Red Beard would let me join your crew . . . for good?"

Wally's tail wagged. The thought of having a new friend on board made him very happy.

"But what about the North Pole?" Wally asked. "Won't you miss your friends here? And your adventures in the snow?"

"I can come back to visit my old friends," Frosty said. "And if I joined your crew, I could make so many new ones!" The little pup sighed. "I love exploring, but I hate the cold. Even with my new jacket. I don't think I'll ever feel like I'm part of the action here, you know?"

Wally *did* know. Not long ago, *he* was the pup hoping for a new life filled with friends and adventure. He understood how Frosty felt. And he wanted to be able to share his pirate life with a new friend. He was sure Frosty would love the high seas and life on the *Salty Bone*.

And after the Great Ice Race, Frosty already seemed like part of their crew.

As soon as Captain Red Beard heard the idea, he leaped up and howled. "Of course this pup can join me crew! Christmas is all about giving, right? So let's give him the whole ship! I'll give him my job as captain, too!"

Curly stepped forward and said quietly, "Er, maybe the best gift for Frosty would be the gift of pirate *training*? Wally could help him learn the ropes as a cabin pup, and we can see how it goes from there."

"Yes," Red Beard said. "Yes, just like I said. I think perhaps he should start as a cabin pup." Then he spun in a happy circle and raced toward the door. "Now that our bellies are full and our tails are waggin', it's time for us to return to our ship, me crew! Our next adventure awaits."

As everyone said their goodbyes, Henry pulled Wally aside. "Hey, mate, I have a little something for you." He handed Wally a gift wrapped in brown paper. "It's not fancy, but I hope you'll like it."

"I have something for you, too!" Wally said. He dropped the book of photos in Henry's lap.

The two friends opened their gifts at the same time. "It's a book of stories I wrote!" Henry told Wally. "I wrote about some of our best adventures—the treasure hunt on Boneyard Island, the battle against the Sea Slug, that time we were prisoners on the kitten pirate ship. It's all in there! I can read it to you before bed sometimes. The only thing I haven't put in there yet is our trip to the North Pole."

That's when Henry opened the book from Wally. He laughed when he saw the pictures of their North Pole journey. "You made a book about the Great Ice Race?" He patted Wally on the back and said, "I guess we had the same idea, eh? In case you were wondering? Great minds— and best mates—think alike!"

As the puppy pirates padded back to their ship, Wally nuzzled his head against Henry's leg. Just ahead of him, Millie and Stink sang a song. Behind him, he could hear the pugs telling Frosty about their next prank. Wally thought about how lucky he was to have such good friends. They had been on many adventures together, and the best part was, there were more to come.

Wally was certain that having great friends was the greatest gift of all!

**Turn the page for more
Puppy Pirate fun and adventure!**

How to Draw a Puppy Pirate!

Follow the steps below to draw a favorite Puppy Pirate—Frosty!

Step 1: Draw a Christmas tree with the top cut off for the head and body. Add two triangles for the ears and two triangles for the legs.

Step 2: Add another triangle for the nose and a zigzag line down the middle of the body. Now that you have the basic shapes in place, you can add curves and feet to make your drawing look more realistic.

Step 3: Add eyes, a mouth, toes, and a tail. You can draw another triangle on the blanket for the patch.

Step 4: Continue adding details like wrinkles, stitching, and Frosty's black-and-white patches. Now you have a finished drawing of Frosty!

Mrs. C.'s Secret Message

Happy holidays! Mrs. C. has left Wally a special holiday message. Put your knowledge of *Race to the North Pole* to the test by helping him decode it. You can use a notebook or make a copy of this page if you don't want to write in your book.

1. Wally is a soft golden _ _ _ _ _ _ _ _ _ puppy.

   ☐ ☐ ◯ ☐ ☐ ☐ ◯ ☐ ☐

2. _ _ _ _ _ _ and her sister, Puggly, play a prank with a crate of steaks.

   ☐ ◯ ◯ ◯ ☐ ☐

3. The race takes the puppy pirates through Candy Cane _ _ _ _ _ _ .

   ◯ ◯ ☐ ☐ ☐ ◯

4. To win, the puppy pirates must cross the rainbow-colored Snow Cone _ _ _ _ _ _ _ _.

○ □ □ □ ○ □ □

5. The race ended in a tie when the puppy pirates and the North Pole Racers crossed the _ _ _ _ _ _ line at the same time!

○ □ ○ ○ □ ○

Now look at your answers above. The letters that are circled spell four words—but those words are scrambled! Unscramble the letters to complete the final puzzle.

There is nothing better than

_ _ _ _ _ _ _ _ _ _ _ _ _ _!

Present Delivery Race!

Help Santa get presents from his workshop to children and puppies all over the world!

You will need:

Empty boxes covered in wrapping paper (Make sure there are at least three boxes for each team. It's better if the boxes are all different sizes.)

A large, empty room or space

At least four players

How to play:

1. Split into two teams: Team Puppy Pirates and Team North Pole Racers.

2. Split each team into two groups. Half of each team should stand at one end of the room. Give one member from each team three boxes stacked on top of each other. Make sure each person has boxes of different sizes.

3. The other half of each team should stand at the other end of the room.

4. Ready, set, go! Balancing the boxes in one hand, players must walk across the room toward their teammates as quickly as they can without dropping a box. If they drop a box, they must go back to the starting line and try again.

5. When players reach the other side of the room, they must pass the boxes to their teammates. Balancing the boxes in one hand, teammates then walk as quickly as possible back to the other side of the room. Again, if a box is dropped, that player must start over.

6. Play continues until all team members have successfully carried the boxes back and forth across the room. The team to finish first is the winner!

Want to make it harder?
Add a new box to the stack every
time a player passes the presents
to a teammate.

All paws on deck!

Another Puppy Pirates
adventure is on the horizon.
Here's a sneak peek at

Lost at Sea

Captain Red Beard was fighting with the ship's huge wheel. "Blimey!" he shouted, pushing it to port. Then, "*Arrrf!*" He swung the wheel to starboard, and the ship lurched with him.

"What's happening, Captain?" asked Henry in alarm. The boy peered out to sea. "Are we under attack?"

"Me compass!" Red Beard howled. "It's goin' crazy!"

Wally climbed into the steering cabin. He studied the huge compass their captain used to navigate. Usually, the compass needle pointed due north at all times.

But at that moment, the needle was wiggling and wobbling all around the face of the compass. One second it was pointing north, then it swished to point east, then it spun around to point west. To avoid the Triangle, they had to sail north. So every time the needle moved, the captain spun the steering wheel to follow it. All that crazy steering was making the boat zigzag through the water.

"In case you were wondering? This isn't good," Henry said, studying the compass. "It seems to be broken."

"What happened?" Curly asked. She hopped up onto a stool and studied the broken tool. "The compass needle is always supposed to point north. It shouldn't be moving around like that."

Spike wailed. "Nooooooo!"

"What's wrong, Spike?" Wally asked.

"Old Salt's story must be true. I bet we sailed into the Triangle!" Spike whined. "Our compass is broken. We are going to be lost at sea forever. We be dooooomed!"

The rest of the crew began yapping and barking nervously. Old Salt stood quietly, gazing out to sea. Wally thought the strong, old pup looked a little worried, but that couldn't be right. He was the calmest, surest pup Wally had ever met.

"We didn't sail into the Triangle," Curly promised. She turned to the rest of the crew and said loudly, "We *won't* be lost at sea forever. Even if we *had* sailed into the Triangle, there's no truth to all those silly stories. There's just something funny going on with our compass."

"I don't think it's funny," Captain Red Beard growled. He tugged the wheel left, and the ship lurched again. "Not funny at all."

Excerpt copyright © 2019 by Erin Soderberg Downing
and Robin Wasserman. Published in the United States
by Random House Children's Books,
a division of Penguin Random House LLC, New York.

New friends. New adventures.
Find a new series . . . just for you!

ISADORA MOON

ISADORA MOON
Goes to School

Harriet Muncaster

For ballerina and fairy and vampire lovers

COMMANDER IN CHEESE

COMMANDER CHEESE The Big Move

Lindsey Leavitt

For adventurers

JULIAN'S WORLD
THE STORIES JULIAN TELLS

JULIAN'S WORLD
THE STORIES JULIAN TELLS

Ann Cameron

For storytellers

PUPPY PIRATES

PUPPY PIRATES
Stowaway!

Erin Soderberg

For dog lovers

PuRRmaids

PuRRmaids

For mermaid and cat lovers

BALLPARK Mysteries

BALLPARK

RHCB **RHCBooks.com**